IF YOU SCREAM, YOU WILL DIE

Chad Sides

Dragonswalk
Publishing

Also from Chad Sides

The Nightmare After Christmas

Teaching the Wisemen

Published in association with Dragonswalk Publishing.

Publisher's Note: This book is a work of fiction. Names, characters, places, and incidents are either a product of the author's imagination or are used fictitiously. Any similarity to people living or dead is purely coincidental. Printed in the United States of America

ISBN 979-8-9899462-3-5

For Mallory, my biggest fan and the reason these stories are finally getting published.

If You Scream, You Will Die

I would never have admitted this to my father or my brother during even the best of times, but the barn out back always creeped me out a little. I played in it like any dutiful sibling would when brother John beckoned: hide-and-seek, haystack-diving, and dodge-poo, my least favorite because it usually involved me getting pelted with goat turds after calling my brother "John Boy" - we had a myriad of games to keep ourselves amused on a farm that was all adult farm-hands and no other children.

Not all of my memories of that place are bad, but even amongst the good times were the shifting shadows and strange noises that made me want to avoid the barn as much as I could. As I got a little older, I jumped at shadows less but slowly became aware of a subtle yet penetrating feeling of something amiss – something that lurked only at the edge of my consciousness until the full reality of it confronted me like a secret stalker stepping from the shadows to wrap a constricting arm around my neck.

I didn't hate life on the farm in those early days. I didn't have video games like the kids at school, but I had my own horse. Prince Charming was fit and gorgeous enough for competition though I was not. My congenital deformities limit what I can do physically. Mama would tell me I was pretty just the same, but my father was slow with comfort or compliments. I think he was afraid to touch me, which resulted in him attempting to show affection though gifts.

That's why I ended up with the most beautiful horse on the farm. It's why a custom saddle was built to keep me secure atop the Prince's back. I would never run as swift as the wind with him no matter what kind of saddle I had, but I could ride without assistance as long as I was cautious, which I always was.

I had to mount and dismount Prince Charming in the stables using a platform with carefully placed grips which allowed me to use my arms to lower or lift myself without human assistance. This method was not without its dangers. If the Prince were to move, much less get spooked, I could easily be injured or even killed. It was a risk I was always willing to take, and my steed and protector seemed to sense my faith in him. He would remain patiently still until I was firmly in place or safely on the platform.

Because of the presence of my Prince, the stables instilled a sense of safety in me. "Why couldn't we play here?" I often wondered, but my brother always insisted on the barn, maybe for the very reason that it bothered me.

From the door of the stables I could see that other foreboding building, but here it could not touch me. Here I was invincible. And so I remained, even when things began to change, until the death of my Prince.

At some point, I can't say for sure exactly when, I began noticing a coldness in my mother. Once complementary and affectionate, she became distant, speaking to me without actually engaging in conversation. She wasn't cruel, in fact I can't remember her saying an unkind word to me; she just acted like interacting with me was something she had to do instead of something she wanted to do.

I have wondered if that was the result of my father who became increasingly irritable with everyone. I could hear him arguing with the hired help more and more frequently. It got so bad that no one he hired stayed on for very long until he had trouble finding anyone to fill the positions. The buildings began to fall into disrepair.

As unpleasant as all that was, it was my brother who bothered me the most. Our playtime became less and less enjoyable as he developed a mean streak. His pranks became painful although he avoided leaving any marks that might draw the attention of our parents. I no longer liked spending time with him, but I never imagined he would go as far as he did. I could never have fathomed the part any of my family members would play on the worst day of my life; at least at the time it was the worst day.

"Come on, let's play in the barn," John urged.

"No, you're just gonna throw goat crap at me again," I whined.

"I won't! I swear! Come on!"

I gave in and reluctantly followed him wishing instead to be with my Prince. I had already asked one of the few remaining hands to saddle him up for me. I would play whatever stupid game my brother wanted to for a few minutes then find an excuse to slip away and ride. I was afraid that if I didn't humor him at least for a bit he would play some disgusting or painful prank on me.

"I guess. What do you want to play today, Hide and Seek? We are not playing What's That Smell? again!"

As we stepped into the thin shadows of the barn, he turned to me with a look in his eyes I'd never seen before despite all of his mean pranks over the past year or so. "Let's play doctor."

"I don't know how to play that. What do we do, pretend to take out each other's internal organs?"

"Kind of. You take off your clothes and I'll examine you," he replied with a grin that made me nauseous.

"Take off my... you mean just my shoes and jacket, right?"

"That's no fun, you dweeb. You have to take everything off. Or else it's no fun."

"It doesn't sound very fun to me either way. I'm gonna go ride Prince Charming."

My world changed the moment he grabbed my arm. The unthinkable conviction that he did not intend to let me leave knotted my stomach. I cursed myself for letting my eyes tear up. I had neither the strength nor the leverage to pull myself free from his grasp.

"No! Let go! I don't want to play this game!" I yelled.

His grip tightened proving just how strong life on a farm had made him as he had grown. "I think you'll like it," he said in a voice that was almost a growl.

"No! Please! I don't wanna!" I was crying openly now, all the while hating myself for my weakness.

"If you scream you will die," he said as he wrenched my arm. He leaned in to kiss me or lick me or something else he had no chance to do because I clamped my teeth down on the tip of his nose and bit hard enough to draw blood.

John screamed hurling profanities with his mouth as he also hurled me across the floor with his arms. I hit hard enough to make my head swim for a moment, but adrenaline pushed me to move. Still crying but determined, I clambered as best as I could towards the barn door praying for safety out in the open where someone might notice what was happening.

My brother growled something I couldn't make out as he stalked towards me. I was so close to the door; I had to reach it! And when I knew I wouldn't, I began to scream with all the volume my lungs could muster. As he closed in on me, my screams began to dissolve once more into sobs which did not have the volume to reach anyone that hadn't already heard me.

A shadow moved outside. I tried to call for help again but choked on the words. Through my blurred vision, the shadow materialized into the form of my Prince Charming. As if possessed by the spirit of a guardian angel, his eyes glared at my attacker.
With a snort and a whinny that I can only describe as righteous fury, he reared up on his hind legs to bring his front hooves down close enough to allow me to dart behind them - if you can truly call my movements "darting."

Temporarily blocked, my brother paused to yell, "Out of my way, stupid animal!"

The Prince did move but only enough to remain a barrier between my brother and me as I worked my way behind my protector. I would swear he was staring my brother down almost as if daring him to do something. And do something he did; he lashed out to strike Charming in the face. My Prince responded by knocking the little man to the ground and trampling him under hoof.

My screams had brought no one but Prince Charming. My brother's screams brought everyone with my father in the lead. They ignored my sobs. I wanted to give them the benefit of the doubt and say that they assumed I was crying because of what had happened to my brother, but even when I tried to give a full account of the events and why Prince Charming had done what he did, they wouldn't listen. Either they genuinely didn't care or they had decided that I must be lying to stop what was coming next. But I didn't know what was coming next, not until I saw my mother return from the house with my father's shotgun.

"No!" I screamed bawling even harder than I had when it was my life on the line. "You can't do it! Please, don't!"

My pleas went ignored as my father coldly stepped up to my horse, put the barrel of his gun against my Prince's temple, and ended the magnificent protector's life for daring to save mine.

I was inconsolable for some time after that. I only vaguely remember my brother being in the hospital. His legs had been crushed requiring physical therapy and leg braces. The doctors said he would walk again on his own after some time, but when I left home, he was still in the braces.

I was too young to leave home immediately. The only place I could go to get away from home was school. That became my haven.

I'd never been part of the popular crowd, never invited to the parties, and even if I had been I wouldn't have dared allow myself to become inebriated amongst a crowd not known for discretion or acceptance of those who were different. So I never sought to numb my pain with beer or drugs. If I might have ever considered trying such things to fit in, my desire for solitude pushed me away from interacting with anyone, bad influences or good.

What else is a person who doesn't play sports and doesn't want social interaction at school going to do if not study? And so I buried myself in books. I quickly rose from an average student to having perfect grades. My initial dreams of being a vet shifted to biochemistry. I have never quite understood what it was that changed my mind, the pain of my loss perhaps, but once on my new course I never looked back.

When I was accepted into college with a full scholarship, I left home with nothing but a suitcase intending to never speak to my family ever again. I was able to live on campus thanks to the assistance program at my school and thus did what even my mother in her most supportive years had told me was impossible: I lived independent of my family.

College was far kinder to me than high school partly because of my study habits and partly because of the exposure to people who wanted to be there to learn. Though I was not ready to date just yet, I had friends for the first time. They became my siblings. Their acceptance was voluntary rather than forced upon them because we were blood, and as the security of their love entrenched itself in my soul, the nightmares of the farm began to fade. I could almost believe that I would eventually reach a point at which I had chased all but the faintest memories from my mind.

A single phone call brought me back to reality. I hadn't spoken to him in over three years and yet I knew it was my father even before he spoke.

"It's been a while," he said in a gruff staccato.

I told myself to be civil, but the words "not long enough" were out of my mouth before I could stop them.

"How's school?"

"Dean's list every year. I'm in the running for valedictorian."

"You need to come home." His tone was demanding. After all that had happened, this was all I got? No apology, no "please," not even so much as a "how are you" or "good job having exceptionally good grades in a difficult course of study."

My simple, curt "no" was as cordial as I could manage.

"Don't be selfish."

"I'm hanging up now."

"Your mother's dying," he blurted before I could shove a dial tone in his face. He finally had my attention, and I felt only a brief moment of shame at being disappointed he hadn't said he was the one dying.

"I..." I began but stopped. My conflicting emotions rendered me speechless. She hadn't been the one to attack me, she hadn't been the one to shoot my Prince Charming in front of me, and yet she was still complicit in my pain.

When it became clear I wasn't going to be able to find the words I needed, my father spoke up. "She wants to see you one last time. You need to come home."

"Will John..." Just saying his name gave me a moment's pause. I tried to cover it by clearing my throat. "...be there?"

"Of course he'll be here. He lives here. He wants to see you."

"I will come on the one condition that he stays the hell away from me."

"He's your brother."

"I mean it. I own a taser. If he is in the same room as me I will fry his nuts." I didn't mention that I was also the owner of a Smith & Wesson handgun. I spent no less than one afternoon a week at a target range and was licensed to conceal carry.

"College sure has given you a crude tongue," he replied.

I fought the urge to scream at him. After what he'd done, all he could comment on was my "crude tongue"? Instead I said, "I mean it. He doesn't come near me."

The initial threat had been made off the cuff, but the moment I said the words I knew that I did indeed mean it. I might not actually zap him simply for being in the same room, but I would not allow him to touch me. And not only that, I would have my firearm with me. At the first hint of playing "doctor," getting tased would be the least of his worries.

"Fine. Have it your way. I don't know why you got to be so difficult about it."

I was too weary to care if he was that oblivious or if he was being willfully obstinate. Not that it mattered. I would say my goodbyes out of respect then walk away for the final time. I barely had it in me to care that my mother was on her deathbed; the rest of them could rot.

The nightmares plagued me once more that night. In them my father shot Prince Charming as everyone else laughed. John was not trampled but on his feet with the rest of them. He even kicked the corpse of my Prince a few times just to goad me. Then they all advanced towards me chanting "let's play doctor!" I awoke with a scream when they reached out to grab me.

Chest heaving, heart pounding, pores gushing sweat I couldn't bring myself to lay back down much less relax enough to sleep. Instead I turned on every light in my tiny apartment daring a shadow to show itself. When I sat down again, I had both hands wrapped around a small glass of pinot noir.

I stared at nothing in an effort to allow the vestiges of the dream to fall from my mind without triggering any memories. Drops of rain hitting the window made me jump. Only when the sound became a steady patter did my mind stop trying to convince me that someone was actually tapping on the glass perhaps with the intention of smashing through.

At some point in my rattled state I must have managed to fall asleep because in the blink of an eye light from the sun warmed my face. I felt better than I'd expected until I moved and realized that the position I'd been in was not ideal for sleeping and had resulted in a tight muscle in my neck. I immediately felt tired again but resigned myself to the tasks ahead. The second of them would be pleasant at least, for after making my flight plans I intended to meet with my closest friends. I didn't feel comfortable returning home without someone knowing where I was going and when to expect me back.

Sammi and Jerry met me later that morning at our usual coffee shop. I knew they would both insist on going with me, which they did, but I refused. I told them I needed to do this on my own. The truth is that I was both embarrassed by my family and terrified of subjecting the people I considered to be my true family to the horrors of those related to me. I think deep down I harbored a fear that by seeing where I came from their opinion of me would change even if only on a subconscious level.

I ensured they both had the address of the house and the phone number there. I also made sure I had both of their numbers written down on paper in case I found myself without cell service and unable to look up the contact information on my phone.

With my preparations made and my spirits a little higher thanks to the company and coffee, I returned home to pack. I retrieved my Smith & Wesson first. Although I'd cleaned it recently I felt better once I'd double-checked it. I packed it carefully in a hard-shell, cushioned case according to airline laws. I feared this above all else being lost or confiscated. This was my courage. I'd followed all the proper guidelines, but letting it go meant there was a chance I wouldn't get it back.

I confirmed my taser was fully charged with new batteries, safely stored in its own case, and tucked in with my clothes. Having my two weapons packed and checked separately gave me some comfort since I could still have access to one if something happened to the other, but the taser would never give me the same sense of control as the handgun.

Sammi drove me to the airport and helped me get my luggage, as minimal as it was, to the baggage check. We parted with one last plea to not go alone and a lingering hug as I tried to absorb as much emotional strength as I could. I soon realized just how much I had needed that as my apprehension grew to the point of nausea once I was boarded. I tried to lose myself in the writings of Harper Lee only to find it necessary to read the same page two or three times to retain it.

I was sure I would have to run to the lavatory to vomit as we began our descent and only felt better when I had my hands on both my bag with the taser and the case with the Smith & Wesson. I tucked the case into my bag to ensure no one would know I had it. And just in time because moments later I heard my brother calling my name. I cursed quietly knowing that I wouldn't have a chance to prepare either weapon now without being seen. I considered ducking into a bathroom stall but decided I didn't want to risk being stopped and disarmed by security before leaving the airport.

John insisted on carrying my bag despite my protest that I could use a cart to transport it without his help. "You take too long," he said. Before I could reply that I'd rather take a taxi anyway and then he wouldn't have to wait on me, he had started walking away. I couldn't catch up, much less take my bag back by force. I had to decide which was worse: being manhandled like this or leaving John alone with my bag. The former was distasteful; the latter was unthinkable. I resigned myself to chase after him while reminding myself that after this visit I'd never have to see him again.

John tossed my bag in the bed of the truck then climbed into the cab without offering me any help getting in myself. I was irritated and breathing heavily from struggling to keep pace with him until I realized this was my chance to get even if only in a small way. He would not wish to explain why he had my bag but not me so he would neither leave me nor allow anything to happen to me. He wouldn't think to remove my bag from the truck in order to cover his tracks therefore he wouldn't chance anything to be covered. And so I took my time. With each impatient "hurry up" he hurled at me I smiled a little more.

He made a few pitiful attempts at conversation during the drive, but I said little. At first I found it amusing to frustrate him. My mood changed to quiet apprehension when I considered that I had never given anyone in my family my flight information.
How had John known when to be at the airport? My mind conjured a few innocuous explanations which involved someone in the household making accurate

deductions about the most obvious airport I would use which would have information on flights coming in, and yet I couldn't help but worry that they were getting information about me from some unknown source.

I imagined John sensing my new found discomfort and taking the same joy in it that I had taken in his frustration. Could he read my expression without needing to look directly at me? Why did he keep glancing at me? "Keep your eyes on the road!" I wanted to yell at him. Would that draw his attention to me even more?

Sweat dampened my forehead, but all I could do was try to settle my mind. I concentrated on breathing slowly and told myself to not give him the satisfaction of seeing me bothered. I endured the rest of the ride huddled against the door while trying not to look like I was cowering.

I barely recognized the farm. Crumbling ruins poked out here and there from among the growing bushes and saplings. Fields where livestock once grazed now held only tall weeds surrounded by shards of broken fences. I felt like I was looking at the broken bones of a decaying corpse.

The only structure that didn't look completely neglected was that ugly barn. I wondered if anyone had so much as stepped foot past it in the years I'd been gone.

Even the house appeared to be on the verge of being condemned. The front porch had partially collapsed, shingles were missing from the roof, windows were broken and poorly patched with plastic that couldn't possibly keep out the rain.

The front yard wasn't as overgrown as the fields, but, like the house, it seemed to get minimal attention. The path to the barn, on the other hand, was well worn. My father or brother, maybe both of them together, must have put a workshop out there. Did it occupy so much of their attention that they couldn't be bothered with anything else?

I saw no indication of what projects they might use to busy themselves, but my curiosity was fleeting. I was here to pay my respects to my mother, then I would leave for the last time. I had no father. I had no brother. I'd rather not know anything about their interests and hobbies.

The decay around me made me all the more eager to get away from this place. I couldn't imagine how things had gotten so bad so quickly. Had the place been in worse shape than I'd realized before I left? John walked with a pronounced limp now, but otherwise he seemed fit and healthy; he showed no signs of being incapable of working. For all his faults, my father had been a hard worker. Was his health failing? There had to be some explanation as to why he was letting the place fall apart.

When we pulled to a stop in front of the house my father stood waiting for us. He was so quick to pull open my door that for a brief moment I thought I might fall out of the truck. "'Bout time you made it home," he said, barely loud enough for me to hear.

"I had to leave home to come here," I replied.

John grabbed my bag out of the bed of the truck. "I can get that," I tried to say, pushing my way past my father. He stepped in front of me.

"Your mother has been asking for you."

"Then I'll go see her."

"She's asleep right now."

"Then why bring it up? Why not wait until she's ready to tell me she wants to see me?" John was inside the house with my bag. I was angry that they thought I couldn't handle my own luggage. I would find a way to show them I wasn't as weak as they thought I was.

"You forget your manners in college? Go wash up. We'll have some dinner. Your ma will be up by then. You can stay in your old room."

My anger tempted me to argue with him just out of spite, but I was too eager to be reunited with my bag. My intent to use the taser on my brother was not idle; I wanted it in my hand, and I wanted it now.

Anxiety shot through me when I remembered that I had mentioned the taser to my father. Had he told John? Was this show of help all to separate me from my bag so that John could confiscate my weapon? The gun! Had I laid it on top or stuck it under my clothes? I had to get to my room before John had a chance to rifle through my stuff!

I cursed my deformed legs as I did my best to hurry to my room. John better not utter one word of complaint about his limp in my presence. He had no idea what real struggle was.

I met my brother in the hallway outside my room.

"You're in there."

"Yeah, I know."

"Bathroom lock don't work. There's a sign to hang on the door so people know not to walk in on you."

It probably doesn't work on purpose, I thought. I was certain there would be no lock on the bedroom door, either. There never had been, so why would they add one if they weren't willing to fix the existing one for the bathroom? I had nowhere to go where I could have any security at all. That made me yearn for a weapon at hand all the more.

"I'm going to rest a little before supper. Flying always tires me out, you know." If he could tell I was lying he didn't care. He muttered something about seeing me in a while and walked away. I hurried into my room and shut the door.

Alone at last! I let out a sigh that was dangerously close to a sob. I tossed my bag on the bed and tore it open. Oh, thank God! My taser and gun were still there! Relief washed so much tension out of me that I sank to the floor where I sat for several minutes not moving, just relishing the feel of the taser against my fingers and knowing that the Smith & Wesson was within reach.

I looked at my weapons for a moment reconsidering my options. The gun was too bulky to wear around the house without being obvious. If either of the men felt threatened they might feel the need to show their strength. The dominance I had experienced so far was aggravating but not dangerous. If I pushed them into a need to act, I might be putting myself in unnecessary danger. If I ventured outside, I could justify having a firearm. Inside the taser would suffice.

Besides, surely John wouldn't try anything in here around our parents. Who was I kidding? We weren't children anymore. I would never forgive him for what he did, but that didn't mean he would do something like that again even if he had the chance, especially with his own mother dying in the same house. Paranoia: that's all it was.

A knock at the door startled me. "Dinner."

No, I was in no danger. I would be in a crowd, at my mother's bedside, or in my room with the door closed at all times. I wouldn't give John the chance to try anything, he would mind his own business without easy prey, and I would leave this place for the last time satisfied that I'd done the right thing by paying respects to my mother.

I slipped the taser into my pocket before opening the door.

The kitchen and dining room were surprisingly tidy compared to the disarray outside. This was my mother's realm. I could tell that the rooms hadn't gotten much attention lately, but that looked like the neglect of a couple of weeks rather than a few years. The place was dusty, dishes sat in the sink, and the counters needed a scrub. I wouldn't normally have expected my mother to live in filth, but I also wouldn't have expected my father to let the house fall apart. Seeing that I was not sharing my dining space with a family of roaches made me feel better about eating there.

Supper was an unappetizing combination of a can of off-brand pasta in a bland meat sauce, a can of green beans, and a can of creamed corn which was the only thing that tasted halfway decent. I sat as far away as I could from my father and brother who seemed content to sit next to each other. I didn't speak even when spoken to.

My father said, "All right, let's go get your ma up and get some food in her." He sounded frustrated but lightened a little when I stood up.

I dutifully followed, leaving the rest of my uneaten supper on the table. A strange debate flickered through my mind: should I clean up my dishes or leave them? I didn't much care if it bothered anyone but my mother who was beyond such worries, or so my father made it sound. At the same time I didn't want to become that kind of person. I decided to return later and take care of the mess. I might even clean the rest of the dishes just to chase away those petty desires.

The moment I saw my mother any unpleasant thoughts I might have had got washed over with compassion. She looked so frail in her bed with the covers pulled up to her chest. She had one arm under the blanket and one out laid beside her like she should have an I.V. running to it. She was little more than skin and bones.

I took her tiny hand, so weak it almost felt lifeless. How long has she been sick? She'd lost too much weight for this to be sudden. I felt ashamed for cutting my family off so completely.

"Ma? Ma, are you awake?"

"John?"

"No, ma, it's me."

"Where's John?"

"I'm here," he replied as he pushed me out of the way but far more gently than I ever would have expected of him.

"Let's get you fed, ma," he said. He helped her sit up then very carefully spoon fed her creamed corn that one of them had mashed until nothing solid remained of it.

I watched him with my mouth agape. He was so careful, so loving, maybe he wasn't that cruel boy I used to know. My throat grew tight. I fought my tears as I watched them together.

"She doesn't know me," I said quietly.

"She has her good days and her bad ones," my father said from across the room.

Was this the reason the farm was in such bad shape? Were these two spending all their time taking care of my mother? But why not hire somebody else to do the work? Lack of funds? I tried to figure out the most logical answer, but I couldn't think clearly. My thoughts kept returning to the shadow of my mother lying on the bed in front of me.

When John was finished, he backed away almost meekly. For the first time since that day in the barn, maybe longer, I smiled at him. He didn't notice, but that didn't matter. I'd thought I could never forgive him; now, the first hint of doubt peeked in. If he'd become the person I was seeing here then maybe, just maybe, one day…

My mother groaned, drawing my attention back to her. I went again to her bedside and touched her bony hand. "Mama?"

"John?" she mumbled. "Where's John?"

I sat for a while before my father put his hand on my shoulder. He was far rougher than John had been, but I detected no malice in his touch or his tone. "Let her sleep now."

No matter how touched I might have been by the care the two men had shown I was not yet ready for conversation with them. Before they could engage me, I retreated to my room where I could be alone with my thoughts and my sorrow. I'd intended to leave first thing in the morning. Now I wasn't so sure that was the best idea. What if Mama became lucid again and asked for me after I'd left? Even if nobody ever told me that had happened, I would always wonder if it had. She hadn't been there for me when

I'd needed her the most, not in a meaningful way, but that didn't mean I couldn't be there for her.

As I sat on the edge of my bed with my hands clasped together in my lap, I took a good look around my room for the first time since my return. Almost no trace of me remained. The bed was lower to the ground than most, that much was the same, but that was about it.

I'd taken all of the pictures of Prince Charming with me to college. I'd hardly had a picture of me that didn't include him, so I wasn't surprised to not see my face anywhere. But most every other decoration I'd owned had remained here. Now the walls were completely bare save for one small painting of a flower hung above the bed and a round clock that wasn't keeping time.

A chest of drawers and a small table were the only other furniture. I didn't recognize either of them. Both were devoid of any decoration. Maybe such an empty room was simply easier to clean? The place was dusty, but it wasn't disgusting.

In truth, the room had never been full. I have mentioned my father's gifts in lieu of affection, but those tended to be either better suited for a barn than a bedroom or were things that I outgrew. Even so, when I'd left home, some of my academic achievements hung on the walls, a few small pieces of horse memorabilia sat here and there, and other such decorations made the room look lived in. Now the lack of any remnant of me in my own room felt like a mocking gesture.

As I imagined what the room had looked like, memories of the Prince flooded into my mind. I could see myself riding atop his strong back. That made me think of my mother at a time when I felt like she would always be the one person I could count on.
Feelings of loss wrapped fingers around my heart and squeezed. I desperately needed some connection to those happy memories. I glanced again around my barren room; no such connection remained here.

Despair brought me to the verge of tears until the obvious answer hit me: my saddle! Even if I could somehow have taken it to college with me, my dorm room had been far too small for it. Might it still be here?

My enthusiasm drained away when I thought about where I would have to look for it: that damned barn. What was stronger, my aversion to that hellish place or my desire to connect with the memory of my Prince? Hopefulness and misgivings pulled me one way then another as I considered my options.

Maybe I should ask for John's help? He could be useful, and I wouldn't have to explain myself if anyone saw me. He had been so careful with Mama, maybe he would be with me, too. But, no, if there was any hope that we could one day reconcile, which felt less impossible now than it did yesterday, it was still a long time to come. He and my father both were the cause of my traumas. If I was going to find any comfort around here, it would have to be far away from both of them.

Indecisive about when I should set about my quest or what to do until then but feeling a little better with a course of action in mind, I managed to close my eyes for a short, fitful nap. I awoke with a start, certain that someone was standing over me. I felt like I couldn't catch my breath as I frantically searched the room. I calmed down only when I was certain I was alone, but paranoia insisted that just because no one was here now that didn't mean someone hadn't been.

I carefully cracked open the door of my room and surveyed the hallway outside. Nobody lurked.

This had to stop. I could remain here imprisoned by my anxiety and sorrow, or I could step out to reclaim that connection to the best of the few good memories I had here. I would not be imprisoned.

The weight of my Smith & Wesson felt good as I slid it into my pocket. I mentally ran through my excuse of why I was carrying it in case anyone asked and was surprised to find myself feeling a twinge of guilt. The image of John with Mama crept into my mind and didn't want to leave. Even more than before, I questioned my justification for carrying a lethal weapon. No way would he attempt something that deserved a bullet.

"Let's play doctor." The words broke through like an axe splintering a locked door. I loaded the gun. I would hope to God I didn't have to use it, but I would not leave it behind based on a brief observation of a single gentle moment.

I untied my shoes and retied them tighter, checked the beam of my flashlight, and settled my mind on the possibility that no matter how careful I was someone might confront me. Why should they care that I wanted to see my saddle? If anything they would probably insist on helping just like John had with my bag which had me unsure that I could deter them. I had no qualms about telling them to leave me alone, I just didn't think they would listen. If that happened maybe I could get them to bring the saddle up to my room and leave me be here.

I had to be prepared for a confrontation, but I was going to do my best to avoid one. The window in my room was the first place I checked. I couldn't see the barn from this angle, but the dying light had me hopeful that everyone would be settling in for the night watching whatever TV shows entertained them or taking care of Mama. I would not, however, assume that they were doing any such thing.

Once more I eased my bedroom door open to peek into the hallway. Only when I neither saw nor heard anything did I venture out. My journey through the house was a series of the same cautious steps. At each doorway and every corner I made sure the path ahead of me was clear and that no one was coming up behind me.

Once outside I paused even longer to take in every portion of the backyard and beyond. The overgrown weeds blocked my view in places, but I felt sure that if anything was moving I would see the weeds swaying. I watched the pathway to the barn and the building itself hunting for any sign that someone was heading in that direction or might be about to return from it.

As the sun sank a little lower, I was glad that I hadn't waited any longer to get started. The dim light already obscured the distant details. Soon darkness would hide everything beyond the beam of my flashlight. Planning my adventure was already harrowing enough without having to do it blindly.

My first challenge: I couldn't cross the distance from the house to the barn quickly. Even John with his limp could overtake me at a casual pace and wouldn't have to push himself very hard to catch up if he saw me. I'd be better off if I could remain undetected. Could I hide in the weeds if I heard anyone coming? That was probably a bad idea since I would look suspicious if anything went wrong.

Maybe, though, if I let the darkness deepen and shaded the flashlight with my hand I could avoid being seen at all. They would have no reason to be so stealthy, so I should be able to see them before they saw me.

I didn't have long to wait for the sun to sink below the horizon. I spent those few minutes moving casually towards the path figuring that if anyone came out here it would be easy to explain away being in the yard without revealing my true intentions. If I had to, I could return to my room and come back out when they had lost interest in me again.

Although nobody appeared, I wasn't convinced that no one had seen me. I stood at the mouth of the path telling myself that it was to let my eyes adjust to the dim light, but really I was nervous that at any moment my father would step up behind me asking me what I thought I was doing out here.

Only when my fear of not being able to see rose to the level of my fear of being seen did I venture forth. I had to step carefully using the flashlight only when absolutely necessary to be sure I wouldn't trip. The stars kept the night from being completely pitch dark; otherwise the only light was the little that spilled from the house's windows which was not enough to penetrate the gloom this far away.

I hadn't made it halfway down the path when I had to pause to collect my courage. Gun or no gun being out here with hardly any light among the ruins of a place so overgrown that it was barely familiar to me was creepy. I had to remind myself why I was out here then listen long enough to be absolutely certain nothing was moving in the night before I could bring myself to push onward.

Nothing jumped out. Nothing grabbed me. Nothing so much as startled me. I laughed away my previous fears but allowed myself a moment of triumph as well. I had made it! That was something wasn't it?

Even so, the hard part was still ahead of me. Creatures that might lurk in the night were one thing, but ghosts awaited me inside. There was no escaping those. Confronting them was the price I must pay to reconnect with Prince Charming.

I walked past the main barn entrance. I couldn't help overthinking everything that could go wrong with my little misadventure, and opening the door to find someone there was a fear I couldn't shake. "What are you doing out here at this time of day?" I might be able to bite back a rude reply, but I'd rather not have to.

I did have another reason to go around back, though. Besides the fact that I might be able to create a gap in the sliding door that was large enough for me to squeeze through should the barn turn out to be locked, a customized door had been created for me there.

As a child I couldn't budge the heavy sliding panel on that side of the building. If it was closed, I had to either walk around the building or find someone who could open it. My private door allowed me an exit to reach the stables on the other side more easily. It was one of those "gifts" from my father back when he at least pretended to like me.

I wondered if that vestige of my young life would still be here, and when I saw it, I stood frozen for a long moment letting my fingers rest on the handle. I'd forgotten how small it was. Now that I was older, I wouldn't fit without stooping; anyone larger would struggle. It really was made just for me back when I was younger and untainted. I released a sigh - those were happier days.

I turned around to look at the ruins of the stable. The darkness hid the decay allowing me to imagine it as it once was which brought a smile to my face. I turned back to the door then paused. This was why I'd come out here wasn't it, to reconnect with better times? I leaned my back against the wall of the barn and allowed myself to enjoy the memories.

Wind rustled leaves startling me back to the present. My smile fell away as I considered the current reality. The stables were dead now. The house was dying. When Ma was gone, would the men set about the task of repairs or let it all continue to rot away?

For some reason the only structure that had any sign of life was this barn. Suddenly I was curious to know why. What was in here that made this place worthy of more attention than the building in which they all lived? The time had come to find out.

I was disappointed, though not surprised, to find the door locked. Maybe I could try picking the lock? I patted my pockets as I tried to think of an idea. The jingle of keys caught me off guard. I didn't even remember picking them up.

"I wonder…" I muttered to myself as I retrieved the keys and held them up in front of the flashlight. My jaw dropped. "Sometimes I amaze even myself," I muttered quoting Han Solo, the daring adventure hero who could handle himself in a fistfight or a gun fight.

I had forgotten all about having a key to this door because until a few minutes ago I had forgotten about the door itself. In fact, I had forgotten about it so completely that the more I considered it the more I was certain I'd never taken the key off my ring. Maybe somewhere deep down I always knew I would be back here eventually. Or maybe it was nothing more than a happy accident, one which my subconscious made use of when I absentmindedly slipped the keys into my pocket.

"They probably changed the lock," I muttered, unwilling to accept the good fortune. But they hadn't. My key turned as easily as it ever had.

Maybe I was supposed to be here. I thought back to the scene at my mother's bed, the tenderness I'd witnessed. Were the hint of love there and the sign of life here glimmers of hope for the future of this family?

"You're not the optimistic sort. Why are you all of a sudden so quick to believe anything here could ever end well?" I mumbled to myself. I pondered the question as I eased open the door. Maybe I never would have a loving relationship with my father and brother, but maybe a reason to not hate them would be a pleasant change.

Any hopefulness trying to surface turned to confusion when I smelled the air. Barns smell musty, this one smelled disinfected. Bleach and some kind of pine cleaner fought for control of my senses. Who bleaches a barn?

I still very much intended to find my saddle, but I was increasingly curious about what went on in this place. If I was going to be looking around anyway, there would be no harm in satisfying my curiosity while I was here.

The portion of the barn I'd entered was designed as a garage. It could hold a couple of trucks or tractors and some of the smaller farm equipment during bad weather, but it stayed mostly empty whenever we needed to bring the animals in and out. Now that animals weren't a consideration, I was a little surprised to not find the place filled with junk.

I would not have put it past my father to box up everything missing from my room and leave it here for spiders and summer heat to do with as they wished, but so far nothing at all appeared to be out here. Even the walls beside me were bare: no tools, no shelves, nothing.

I knew the place couldn't be as barren as it felt because at least two different cleaners had been used which meant at least two different surfaces in need of cleaning. Something was here.

The darkness of the garage strangled my flashlight's beam before it revealed any answers. If I wanted to know more, I had to venture further in. If only I could turn on the overhead light, but that would be too easily visible from the house. Now that I was officially snooping, I wanted to avoid attention more than ever.

I made my way towards the barn's center aisle which ran from the garage to the front entrance. On one side of the aisle were stalls for the animals. Facing them were a cluster of rooms. I was surprised to realize that I had very little idea what those rooms were for. John had tried a few times to coax me back there during hide-and-seek, but if the barn was creepy, those mysterious rooms were part of the reason. I'd managed to avoid going back there as a kid, and I had no desire to explore them now in the dark.

One room was the exception to my aversion: the tack room. This was where my saddle, among other things, had been stored and where it was most likely to be kept now if it were still here at all. If I found it, would my growing curiosity about what went on in the barn push me to go in the back? Probably not.

My light reflected off a surface on the other side of the garage. So it wasn't completely empty after all. I told myself I was brave for venturing over to check it out. There was no need to go to the back rooms; I would find out all I needed to in the garage.

A pickup truck, one I'd never seen before, sat against the far wall. It wasn't new, but it looked like it was in good shape, maybe even better than the one John had driven to the airport. The dark red paint faded into the darkness, but I couldn't see any of the dents and dings that covered the other vehicle. "Surface details," I reminded myself. "Just because it looks better on the outside doesn't mean it's any good on the inside."

Another detail caught my eye. This truck had a camper shell. It was painted the same red as the rest of the truck. I tried to peek inside but couldn't locate a window. What I did notice was an Alabama license plate. That was strange considering we weren't anywhere near Alabama.

A bump somewhere in the distance startled me. I'd better get back on task. They had another truck, so what? Maybe fixing it up was what they did here. I saw no sign of a mechanic's tools, but that didn't mean they weren't somewhere out of sight.

I hurried towards the tack room with the sound of the bump still echoing in my mind. The wind maybe? Probably. It sounded like it could have been the hoof of a horse striking the wood of the building, but of course, there were no horses here.
Still, if it turned out to be my father or brother coming

in, my presence in the tack room would be easier to explain away. Easier than what? Than me looking at their truck? Why would they care? Just the same, I'd rather not even have that discussion. Why was I so nervous?

When I reached the stalls I looked over to see what kind of state they were in. This part of the barn I knew well. Each enclosure was divided from the others by a solid wooden wall that rose roughly two-thirds of the way to the ceiling which was the floor of the loft. A four foot high gate allowed entry from the aisle while a door opened to the outside from the middle two.

The smell of disinfectant was stronger here. The odor wafted from the first stall which was so clean I couldn't see any sign that an animal had ever stepped foot inside. Maybe it was being prepped for a renovation? I could tell that something was different further down the aisle, I just couldn't see what it was.

When I reached the first of the middle stalls, my curiosity soured into a sickening feeling. This was beyond weird. A metal frame had been attached to the wooden gate. Attached to that was a portion of chain link fencing interwoven with barbed wire. The open portions of the walls on either side had similar barriers. The fence rose all the way to the ceiling resulting in a completely enclosed space.

The door leading outside no longer existed, and a chain with a padlock looked like it would easily secure the gate against any attempt to open it. Nothing was getting out of this stall.

What did they need a cage like this for? They had no animals as far as I could tell. And besides, what kind of animal needed chain link and barbed wire inside of a stall already built to hold something as large and powerful as a horse?

I risked a look inside. The first thing I noticed was a metal pail sitting in one corner. Across from it a wooden platform extended from the wall. I assumed it to be an oversized shelf until I saw the dingy looking pillow. This was a bed! I stifled a gasp with the crook of my arm.

I tried to conjure a benign explanation for such a bizarre setup. It was the leg iron attached to the wall at the foot of the bed that removed any doubt. This was a cell for a human being, and the only human here they might put into it was me!

The entirety of my visit flashed before my eyes. Was Ma really sick? She wouldn't put on a show to lure me here would she? But that didn't mean my father or my brother wouldn't seize upon the opportunity. They had gone to some lengths to figure out my flight information quite possibly to make sure I rode with John instead of bringing another vehicle I might be able to use to escape. No lock on my bedroom. No lock on the bathroom. I had nowhere safe I could hide. And now I knew that I was never going to leave this barn if they had their way.

Another thud made me jump. I gasped for breath and fought back tears. I had to get out of here! How? There was nowhere I could run to. The closest neighbor was miles away. Even if I could fumble through handling one of the trucks I couldn't get a key without being caught, and if I got caught, I couldn't outrun either of those men on my best day. Curse my slow, twisted body!

Another thud. That definitely wasn't wind. Did they know I was out here? Did they go to my room to grab me, see that I was gone, and set out looking for me?

I came here for you, Ma. You were the lure. You wouldn't save me then and you're the reason I need saving now.

In that moment I hated my mother as much as either of the men. I wouldn't be here if not for her. If she'd just stood up for me! She didn't even know who I was now!

My hands trembled as I carefully closed the gate to the prison cell. I couldn't let them hear me! When the padlock clanked against the wooden post, I had to fight a sob.

I was too out in the open in the aisle. If anyone came in and turned on the light, they would spot me immediately. Hide. I had to hide!

I risked shining my flashlight around me looking for a place to go. I was shaking so violently I had to steady the beam with both hands. The back door felt impossibly far away. Did I dare try covering that distance? I could hide behind the wall of the last stall if someone came in.

No, that was stupid. If they were out here looking for me, the first place they would check would be my door. Oh, God. I hadn't locked it behind me. If they found it open, they would know for sure I was here.

The front door was an even worse idea. If they weren't looking for me, they would use that door. And if both of them were in it together, I would probably find someone at each exit. In either case anyone at the door or walking along the path from the house would spot me immediately.

Heart pounding I stumbled across the aisle into the tack room. I fought against panic and forced myself to close the door gently instead of slamming it. I had to keep my wits about me. My prudence proved its worth when someone entered the barn just as I closed the door.

"I swear to God, John, if you weren't bigger than me now I'd beat your ass red and raw."

It was my father. He sounded like he was thinking out loud, not actually talking to John. If John wasn't at the front door, he was surely at the back.

Hiding instead of escaping had been the right decision. But would that matter in the long run? They would certainly think to look for me in here if I couldn't find a way out. I scanned the walls. No other doors. I was trapped. Panic choked me. I couldn't catch my breath. Nowhere to go, nowhere to hide.

No, I had to at least try to hide. I had to calm down and think. I couldn't do that standing in front of a door they might open at any moment. But where? Against a wall, a work bench. I crawled under trying to squeeze myself into a dark corner, willing myself to become invisible.

I was on the verge of hyperventilating. I couldn't let them hear me; I had to calm down! I tried to breathe slowly but managed only a sob. My heart hammered so hard it hurt. Oh, God, they were going to get me and lock me in that cage, and there would be nothing I could do to stop them from doing whatever they wanted to with me over and over until there was nothing left of me.

"Don't panic! Calm down! If you scream, you will die," I warned myself, biting my lip and squeezing my eyes tight against the escaping tears.

A thump on the wall behind me made me choke on my own breath. Trying not to gag while I stifled my coughs brought fresh tears.

"Please, let me out. Please?"

I couldn't breathe. The faint voice bled through the wall. Who was that? It had sounded like a girl - not a child but young.

"Hello?" I stammered. No response. I tried again a little louder. Still nothing. I dared not raise my voice any further.

What the hell was going on here? Was someone being held prisoner in a back room? Were there more cages back there? I considered the truck again in that context - a tag from another state, a camper shell that had no windows - a kidnapper's vehicle?

A second voice seeped through the walls. "Nobody's coming. We're just... we're going..." the voice dissolved into weeping. How many people did they have caged up in here? I couldn't let myself become one of them. I would not let myself become one of them.

I focused on controlling my breathing and tried to will my racing heart to slow. I couldn't fight them, couldn't outrun them, but I could out think them.Yes, in fact maybe I already had! I chided myself for being stupid when I realized that in my panic I'd forgotten my gun!

Now I was sick with fear that I had dropped it. I groped for it, certain it would be gone. No, it was there! Now I was sure that I had forgotten to load it. I had to check. I ejected the clip. Fully loaded, good. The weapon gave me confidence, not enough to stop me from trembling, but enough to calm me.

My breath hitched when the clip fell out of my shaking hand and hit the floor with a clatter. I scrambled from my hiding place searching the dark floor trying to find where it had landed. I had to have that clip!

The door burst open. John stood silhouetted in the doorframe as he scanned the room. "You," he growled when he saw me.

I couldn't reach the clip. Had I chambered a round already? I couldn't remember. But now John was on top of me! I couldn't move! I didn't realize I'd pulled the trigger until the noise of the gun was echoing in the rafters. When John's eyes went wide, I wondered if he'd recognized the sound or felt the pain first.

"What did you…" His words trailed off as he rolled onto his back and stared at his bloody hands. He tried to sit up, grimaced with pain, and fell back onto the floor.

Even though he wasn't dead, I felt like a killer. I wanted to throw the gun away. It didn't have to be like this. Why couldn't you just leave me alone?

I'd lost sight of the gun's clip. A single bullet in the chamber was more luck than I had expected, but without that clip I had no other protection. I clambered to my hands and knees searching.

Suddenly, I was flying backwards. I hit the ground stunned, not understanding what had happened until I saw my father looming above me.

"You little runt. You killed your brother. The only decent one of the two of you and you done killed him."

I tried to scoot backwards away from him, but there was nowhere to go. He snatched the gun out of my hand.

"I ought to shoot you, kill you with the same gun," he growled. "I wanted you dead when you was born but your ma wouldn't hear it."

He wrapped his hand around my throat. "I tried to do right by your ma - give you that horse and things. Don't much have to worry about that now, do I?"

I clawed at his arm, beat at it with my fist. He was too strong. I groped for a weapon, found the taser I'd brought only as a diversion from the gun, jammed it into his crotch, and hit the switch.

He made a guttural sound as he convulsed, and for a second his hand constricted around my throat so tightly I thought I would pass out. Tighter. I couldn't breathe. Tighter. I struggled to escape his grasp. Tighter. Then he collapsed onto his back pulling me down on top of him, and still I kept the taser pressed to his groin.

I don't know how long I stayed there crying, trying to kill my father with the taser. As I started to regain my senses, I began to wonder how long it took someone to recover from taser shocks. I had to leave before that happened. I closed the door to the tack room behind me then used the padlock from the cage to secure the latch on the door. I didn't have a key to open the lock; I didn't care.

When I called 911, they didn't believe anything I said at first. When I told them John would die without medical attention, they took me seriously enough to send someone out.

I felt numb as the police and an ambulance arrived. One officer approached me while another cautiously searched the shadows around the driveway. I had used the house phone to place the call, so I now sat on the dingy front steps next to the partially collapsed roof trying to answer the questions they asked me. I couldn't understand why they didn't go directly to the barn until I realized that they were having to ask me the same questions multiple times. Finally, one of the officers ventured along the dark path while the other stayed with me along with a paramedic who looked me over.

I had no sense of time so I can only guess that it was a few minutes later when the whole farm erupted in chaos. The officers radioed for backup, called for more paramedics, and began asking me more serious questions. The night was soon awash in flashing colors and uniformed responders yelling to each other.

"Did you save the people in the back?" I asked one of the officers keeping a watch over me - there were always two now who were not letting me out of their sight.

"People in the back?" he questioned. "They're trapped. You have to get them out."

The officer spoke into his radio. "Did you find some people trapped in the back over there?"

"You mean the gunshot victim and the other one?"

"No!" I yelled. "There's people trapped back there! Prince Charming led me to them."

"Prince Charming?"

The bumps in the barn replayed in my memory. The timing drove me to find the cell instead of exploring, the second one sending me to the tack room seconds before being discovered, the last one alerting me to the presence of someone in the back room. I was and am convinced that what I heard were horse's hooves.

I finally gathered my thoughts enough to answer the officer's question. "Prince Charming saved them like he saved me. He led me to them." They didn't seem to understand my answer. At the time I couldn't understand why. It could not have been any clearer.

The radio burst to life. "Oh, God, what were they doing back here? We need paramedics back out here on the double! And, Lieutenant? We're going to need the coroner, too."

I can't bear to read about all that my father and brother did in that barn. I will give my testimony when called to do so, but I will not follow the trial. Among their charges are kidnapping, imprisonment, sexual assault, and a growing number of murder charges. The two people I heard that night were teenagers, a boy and a girl. Both will testify in the trial. I don't want to talk to them because I don't want to know what they endured. I can't handle knowing why my family did this to them. I don't know if they have been told who it was that called the police or what my relationship to their captors is.

My mother died at the same time my father's captives were being granted their freedom. It seems fitting that the last tiny spark of life went out of the farm at the same time the victims of the barn received a new opportunity to live. If my father couldn't love me because I looked different, if my brother saw me as a victim because he thought I was weak, if my mother had seen in me a lost cause because I had needed her help; Prince Charming saw me as strong enough to put a stop to the evil that stole him away from me. I have been told I'm a hero. It's my Prince who is the true hero; I was just there when he needed me, but maybe that's what it is that makes a hero.

About the Author

Written by Chad Sides.

Chad began writing as an award winning poet and transitioned into story telling with rhyming tales of horror. Now he builds horror and fantasy worlds.

Chad braves the working world by day and the depths of his imagination by night. He lives just outside Atlanta with his wife and a house full of four-legged children.

Find him online at chadsides.com, on Instagram and Facebook at chadsides.author, on TikTok at chadsides.author, and on Twitter at authorchadsides.

Acknowledgements

Special thanks go out to my wife Mallory Sides for her tireless efforts with formatting this and all my books and Brooke Jackson for proofreading help (those commas keep killing me).

Coming Soon from Dragonswalk Publishing

What if everything you thought you knew
about zombies was
WRONG?

<u>INFESTATION</u>

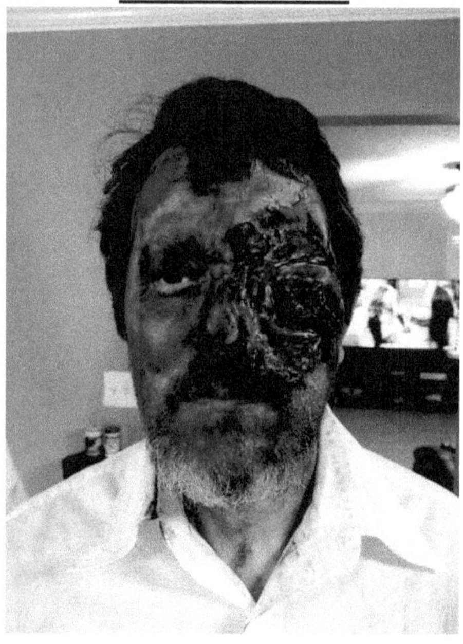